WE REALLY DO CARE

CITY PARK

written by
Tami Lewis Brown

Philomel Books

illustrated by
Tania de Regil

PHILOMEL BOOKS

An imprint of Penguin Random House LLC, New York

First published in the United States of America
by Philomel, an imprint of Penguin Random
House LLC, 2019.

Visit us online at penguinrandomhouse.com

Library of Congress Cataloguing-in-Publication Data is available.

Manufactured in China

ISBN 9781984836304

10 9 8 7 6 5 4 3 2 1

Edited by Jill Santopolo. Design by Jennifer Chung.
Text set in Archer.

For Sarah Davies
—T. L. B.

For Camila and Valentina.
I will always care.
—T. D. R.

My ball belongs to me.

You don't have a ball

and I don't care.

My pets belong to me, too.

You don't have a dog or a cat.
You don't have a fish or a bird.
And I don't care.

Even if you say please, you still can't have my pets.

You can't have my mom.
Or my grandpa.
Or my sister.

You can't even have
my brother!

Wait.

Where is your family?

Are you all alone?
Are you afraid?

Sometimes I'm afraid, too.

Sometimes I'm afraid
I'll lose my toys.

And sometimes I'm afraid I'll lose someone I love.

It's happened to me.
Has it happened to you?

Oh.

Maybe we can share pets.

We can play ball.

And we can even share my brother!

Do you care about me?
Because I care about you.

We care about our mothers and
fathers and sisters and brothers and
all families all over the world.

We care about every land,
every forest, every river, and
every sea.

We care about animals,
big and small, near and far.

And we care about
all children, everywhere.

We care with our voices to shout
and our hands to write.

We care with our arms to lift
and our feet to march.

Our world is our home to share.
Our planet belongs to us all.

We really do care.

Do you?